H●●gs Back Books

– a nose for a good book ...

For my parents, Mavis and Bill – AB
For my Mom – NP

Published by
Hogs Back Books
34 Long Street, Devizes
Wiltshire
SN10 1NT
www.hogsbackbooks.com

Printed in Malta by Melita Press
ISBN: 978-1-907432-36-1
British Library Cataloguing-in-Publication Data.
A catalogue record for this book is available from the British Library.
1 3 5 4 2

Aunt Grizelda's
Fairy Tales
of the
Unexpected

anna best • natallia pavaliayeva

The Princess
and the Frog

Many years ago now,
In a country far away,
There lived a little Princess,
Who was pretty, kind and gay.

It happened that one evening
As she sat beneath a tree,
A small green frog leapt from the lake
And landed on her knee.

It smiled at her politely
And gave a little croak,
Then to her great amazement,
In mellow tones, it spoke:

"Good evening, fair young Princess,
Pray, how are you today?
I hope I didn't startle you
By leaping out that way."

"Oh, not at all," she answered,
Although she felt quite weak,
"But certainly I was surprised
When you began to speak."

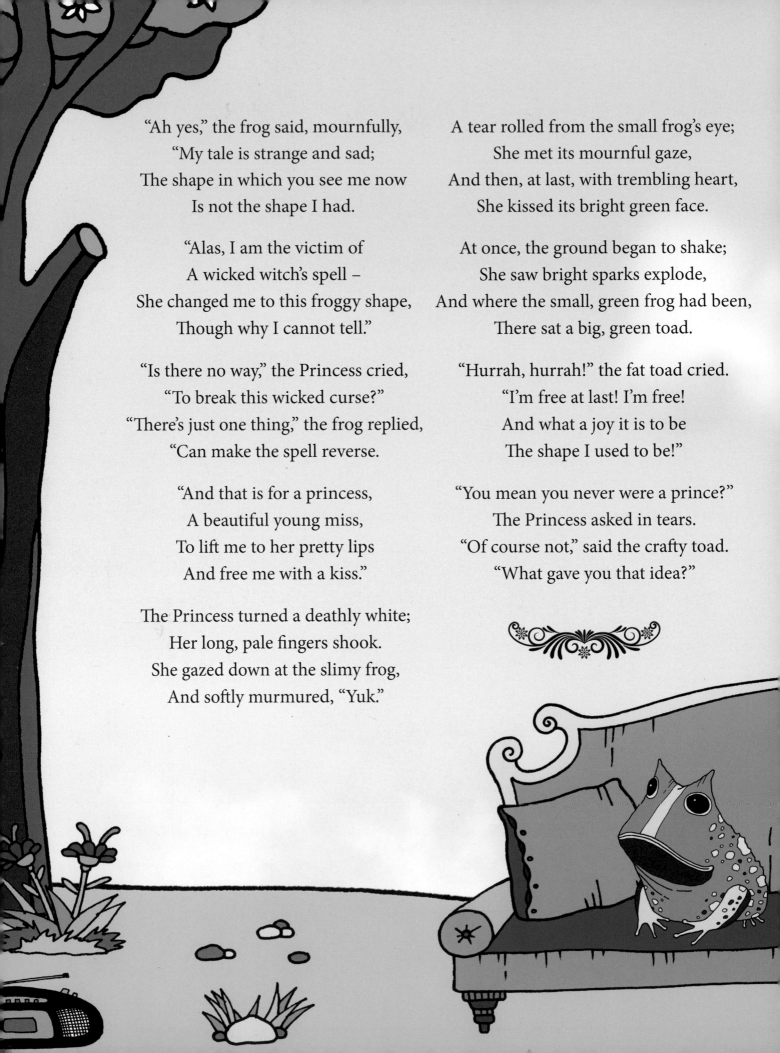

"Ah yes," the frog said, mournfully,
"My tale is strange and sad;
The shape in which you see me now
Is not the shape I had.

"Alas, I am the victim of
A wicked witch's spell –
She changed me to this froggy shape,
Though why I cannot tell."

"Is there no way," the Princess cried,
"To break this wicked curse?"
"There's just one thing," the frog replied,
"Can make the spell reverse.

"And that is for a princess,
A beautiful young miss,
To lift me to her pretty lips
And free me with a kiss."

The Princess turned a deathly white;
Her long, pale fingers shook.
She gazed down at the slimy frog,
And softly murmured, "Yuk."

A tear rolled from the small frog's eye;
She met its mournful gaze,
And then, at last, with trembling heart,
She kissed its bright green face.

At once, the ground began to shake;
She saw bright sparks explode,
And where the small, green frog had been,
There sat a big, green toad.

"Hurrah, hurrah!" the fat toad cried.
"I'm free at last! I'm free!
And what a joy it is to be
The shape I used to be!"

"You mean you never were a prince?"
The Princess asked in tears.
"Of course not," said the crafty toad.
"What gave you that idea?"

Rapunzel

There once was a witch
With incredible power.
She cast a dark spell
And created a tower.
It stretched to the sky,
Thirty metres or more,
But it hadn't a staircase
And hadn't a door.

Then she captured a girl,
And she locked her inside.
(For a fairytale tower
Must be occupied.)

Now the girl, called Rapunzel,
Had very long hair,
Which the witch planned to use
As a long, golden stair.
So, she called to Rapunzel,
"Pray let your hair down.
I've brought you some crisps
From the Tesco in town.

"And be sharp about it!
I haven't much time."
Then without shilly-shally,
She started to climb,
But near to the top,
Her ascent struck a flaw –
The hair came unstuck,
And she crashed to the floor.

Rapunzel peeped down;
On her face a wide grin,
To see the bad witch
Like a crumpled up tin.
"Oh Witchy," she shouted,
"Perhaps I should mention,
The hair wasn't real;
It was just an extension!"

The Twelve Dancing Princesses

Some years ago, or so I'm told,
There lived a grumpy King,
Who never said a cheerful word
Or smiled at anything.
He moaned about the weather
(Much too hot or much too cold).
He moaned about his palace
(Much too big and much too old).
He moaned about his football team
(Why must it always lose?).
But most of all he moaned about
His daughters' ruined shoes.

For every single morning,
When they came to put them on,
The heels were scratched, the toes in holes,
The leather almost gone.
And pairs of shoes, as we all know,
Are dear enough to buy,
But cost becomes excessive
When by twelve you multiply.

"What have you done?" the King would ask,
"To get them in this mess?"
But what had caused the damage,
Not one princess would confess.

At last, the King decided
He must hire a private eye
And found a young man who had been
An international spy.
"And may I ask," the King enquired,
What fits you for this task?"
The young man smiled an impish grin
And said, "Well, as you ask:
I've fought with foreign agents,
Crossed the globe in fighter jets.
I've broken into secret vaults
And leapt off parapets.
I've detonated bridges
And done loads of scary stuff,
So finding what your daughters do
At night can't be too tough."

The King said, "Right, you're hired;
I'll soon end their sneaky games.
And by the way, what is your name?"
The young man answered, "James."

That night, straight after dinner,
All the girls went to their room.
They wore their finest evening gowns
And costly French perfume.
They laughed and chatted gaily
And were blithely unaware
That James was closely watching them
From underneath a chair.

Then suddenly, at eight o'clock,
They pulled a rug aside,
Revealing there a tunnel,
Which they quickly slipped inside.

James followed them with stealthy step
Through passageways of gloom,
Till at the end, revealed at last –
A glorious ballroom!

It sparkled bright with chandeliers;
Fine music filled the space,
And all twelve girls began to dance
Without one scrap of grace.
In horror, James observed them
As they thundered round and round –
The reason for the damaged shoes,
He'd very quickly found!

And there he could have left it,
But the dancing was so grim,
James felt that something must be done,
And it was up to him.
Though there were TV cameras there
(The dance was for a show)
And judges to adjudicate,
Lined neatly in a row,
James chose one of the princesses,
And led her to the floor,
And when he'd waltzed her round the room,
The judges shouted, "More!"

All eyes were pinned upon him
As he gave his demonstration –
His jetés were magnificent;
His pivots a sensation.
The tempo of his cha-cha
Thrilled the audience to bits.
His Charleston left them speechless
As he landed in the splits.
His waltz was simply effortless;
His jump jive was a breeze,
And no one else had ever danced
The rumba with such ease.

The audience was loud with praise;
The judges cried, "Bravo!"
And everyone agreed that he
Must star in every show,
Which James said he'd be pleased to do,
For when all's said and done,
A job on *Strictly* has to be
An awful lot more fun
Than working for a grumpy King,
Who frets and broods about
What his twelve daughters do each night
To wear their shoes right out.

Three Billy Goats Gruff

There were three billy goats called Gruff,
Who lived upon a hill,
And all around the grass grew lush,
And so they ate their fill.
But as they had huge appetites,
In time the green grass vanished
Till only stones and dirt were left,
So soon the three were famished.

The smallest goat said, "Brothers,
We must move to pastures new;
Across the river there are fields
With luscious grass to chew."

The biggest brother gave a snort
And frowned as he replied,
"And how do you propose that we should
Reach the other side?
You see, there is a troll bridge there,
And as you know, a troll
Can eat twelve elephants at once
And swallow them down whole."

The middle brother laughed out loud –
His good sense saved the day.
"A toll bridge, not a troll," he cried,
"We only need to pay!"

LITTLE RED RIDING HOOD

Once upon a wintertime,
Close by a deep, dark wood,
There lived a girl, a little girl,
They called Red Riding Hood.
The child was sweet in every way,
And yet to tell you true,
She had as little common sense
As dumplings in a stew.

Her mother said, "Red Riding Hood,
To Granny's you must go,
But hurry quickly through the wood
And softly, on tip-toe.
For wolves and bears lie sleeping there,
And if you are not quiet,
They may awake and then you'll be
An item in their diet.
And don't forget to charge your phone
And call when you arrive,
For mothers like to be assured
Their child is still alive."

Red Riding Hood she nodded,
Though she hadn't paid much heed.
Her brain was soft as candyfloss
And dandelion seed.
To her the wood looked beautiful;
No danger she espied,
And so, without a trace of fear,
She calmly walked inside.

But deep within that deep, dark wood,
Inside his deep, dark lair,
There lurked a wolf, a big, bad wolf
(What other kind is there?)
He had sharp teeth, sharp, pointy teeth,
Designed to chew and tear,
And brushed them morning, noon and night,
Observing dental care.

But winter had been cruel and long,
And Wolfy had grown thin.
He wanted meat, some proper meat
To sink his canines in.
And not one food delivery man,
With polystyrene tray,
Had dared to drive into the wood
And bring a take away.

Just then, as he gazed out his den,
He saw with greedy eyes
Red Riding Hood approaching him –
At last, a tasty prize!

He stepped straight out and made a bow –
So charming he could be:
"Where are you bound in this dark wood?"
"My Granny's house," said she.
He gasped and faked a frown, and said,
"But dear heart, don't you know,
This place is full of wicked beasts;
Did no one tell you so?"
Red Riding Hood her shoulders shrugged
And smiled a guileless smile.
"Oh, please don't be concerned for me,"
Declared the trusting child.
"For how could there be anyone
Who'd wish to do me ill?"

And Wolfy whispered to himself,
"I think I fit the bill."
But to Red Riding Hood he said,
"Your guardian let me be,
For nothing here can harm you
While you're in my company."

At length, they reached Grandma's abode.
Red Riding Hood walked in,
Close followed by the big, bad wolf,
His face fixed in a grin.
And though he bowed with charming grace,
Old Gran was not deceived
And jumped out of her rocking chair

With super-human speed.
She struck a pose, a fighting pose,
Like Ninja warriors do,
"Get out," she cried, "you wicked wolf,
Or I shall clobber you!"
At first, the wolf was so amazed
He halted in surprise,
But then he started laughing
Till the tears flowed from his eyes.

"How dare you mock my Judo stance?"
Raged Granny in a strop,
And with a blow from her right hand,
She felled him with one chop.

Red Riding Hood shrieked, "Grandmamma,
Poor Wolfy is deceased!"
And Gran replied, quite reasonably,
"I thought that you'd be pleased."

But oh, the girl was filled with grief.
"He meant no harm!" she said,
And sobbing, she dropped to the floor,
Where Wolfy lay stone dead.
"Oh foolish girl!" sighed Grandmamma,
Scolding the weeping child.
"A wolf may wear a smart, dark suit,
But underneath he's wild."

And then she knelt by Wolfy's side
And from his pocket drew
A knife and fork, both razor sharp,
A linen napkin too.
And suddenly the penny dropped:
Red Riding Hood felt shaken –
She'd almost been bad Wolfy's lunch,
But Gran had saved her bacon!

The Princess and the Pea

There was a handsome Prince called Dev;
He'd pots of money too,
But all his blessings couldn't stop
The Prince from feeling blue.
The thing that was upsetting him
And causing such distress
Was simply that he couldn't find
A genuine princess.

He'd sent his courtiers far and wide,
But every girl they found
Was never to the Prince's taste –
Too thin, too short, too round;
Too quiet or too spirited;
Too tiny or too tall;
And not one girl could certify
That she was really royal.

But then, one dark and dismal night
As rain began to pour,
There came the sound of knocking on
The grand old palace door.
The Prince went down to answer it
And found to his surprise
A rain-bedraggled girl, who yet
Held beauty in her eyes.

"Oh, who are you?" Prince Dev enquired.
"I'm Princess Cha," she sighed,
"And if you'd let me shelter here,
I'd really be obliged."
At once, he bade the girl come in,
And when she'd stepped inside,
He hurried to the Queen and said,
"I think I've found my bride!"

The Queen went down to meet her
And exclaimed in tones sincere,
"Let's get you something dry to wear;
You're sopping wet my dear!"
But then she took her son aside
And whispered, "I confess,
She's clearly very beautiful,
But is she a princess?"

"Now luckily, I've got a plan
That will reveal the truth.
A plan that's easy now that she's
To sleep beneath our roof,
For princesses are delicate –
It's just the way they're bred –
And they can feel the slightest lump
Or bump inside their bed."

The Queen took twenty mattresses,
And one upon the other,
She piled them right up to the roof
Then draped them with a cover.
And underneath the bottom one,
She placed a small green pea,
Then whispered softly to herself,
"A princess? We shall see!"

Next morning, in the dining hall,
The royal family waited.
Was Dev to find a bride at last,
Or were their hopes ill fated?
And then, at ten, the girl appeared;
Up to the Queen she stepped,
And said with much annoyance,
"What a night! I've hardly slept!
For something hard kept waking me;
I'm bruised from head to toe.
So if it's all the same to you,
I think it's time to go."

"But wait!" the Queen exclaimed at once.
"The fact you couldn't rest
Has proved beyond a single doubt
You've passed the princess test.

So let the wedding plans begin!
Let's toast this royal romance!"
But Princess Cha replied at once,
"What? Wed your son? No chance!
You're greedy and you're snobbish
And obsessed by high degree.
What fool would marry for a crown,
Instead of love? Not me!"

The Elves and the Shoemaker

There was an old shoemaker lived long ago,
Who worked long and hard at his trade,
But nobody came to his shop anymore,
So, therefore, he didn't get paid.

His wife in despair at their dwindling funds,
Cried out, "Oh, there's ruin in view –
The leather that's left will make one pair of shoes,
Then heaven knows what we shall do!"

The shoemaker stared at his workbench and said,
"My dear, I will do what I can,
But if this last pair doesn't fetch a good price,
I fear I'm a bankrupted man."

He cut out the shoes and set them aside,
Intending to sew them next day,
But deep in his heart, he was sure as could be
That there in his shop they would stay.

Much later that night, on the tiniest feet,
Came two nimble-fingered young elves,
Who gazed in dismay at the horrible shoes,
Displayed on the shoemaker's shelves.

"Oh dear," said the first, "what appalling designs –
So clumpy and frumpy and plain.
I fear if the shoemaker crafts a new pair,
They'll be just as frightful again."

His friend quite agreed, and he nodded and said,
"Let's help the old man boost his trade."
And neatly they fashioned a pair of high heels –
Stilettos exquisitely made.

Next day, when the shoemaker opened his shop,
He gasped in surprise as he saw
The pair of high heels, very stylish and fine,
Placed neatly beside the shop door.

But was he delighted? Oh no he was not.
He wept and he wailed in dismay:
"There's no one could walk in creations like these!"
And straight off, he threw them away.

The elves, who were spying from under the eaves,
Were very annoyed, and one said,
"Why did we waste time on that thankless old man?
Let's start our own business instead."

And so the two elves grew both happy and rich,
Creating with flair and with passion,
For each shoe they made was a quality shoe,
And quality's always in fashion.

"But what of the shoemaker?" I hear you cry:
He lived with his wife in great need.
He lost job and home, and the reason is this:
He couldn't accept a good deed.

Cinderella

Once upon a time there was
A girl called Cinderella,
Whose wicked sisters made her sleep
On straw down in the cellar.
They called her names and mocked her,
But what was really mean –
They played games on their smart phones
While she was made to clean.

One day while Cinderella
Was polishing the floor,
She heard the doorbell ring
And a knocking at the door.

"Go answer it!" her sisters cried,
"You lazy, useless thing."
And so she did and found it was
A herald from the King.
He played a fanfare loudly,
Then made his proclamation:
"The Prince invites you to a ball.
Please join the celebration!"

"Oh joy!" screeched Cinders' sisters
Rushing over to the door.
"This ball will be more wonderful
Than any held before,
For rumour says the Prince is keen
To end his single life,
And from the ladies at the ball
Will choose himself a wife."

"How cool is that?" said Cinders,
Assuming she could go.
"It's not for you," her sisters cried.
"You've jobs to do, you know –
You've beds to make and floors to vac;
The oven needs a clean.
And how could someone dressed like you
Join such a stately scene?"

At last, the great day came around
As all great days must do.
The ugly sisters hurried off,
Prince Charming to pursue.

Meanwhile poor Cinders closed the door
And went to fetch her broom,
When all at once a mighty flash
Exploded in the room.
Then as the smoke began to clear,
A fairy came in view,
With magic wand and shiny wings,
And heart both kind and true.

"I am your Fairy Godmother,"
She straight away declared.
"And you are going to the ball,
So let's get you prepared."
She waved her magic wand three times,
And Cinders' ragged clothes
Turned to a silken ball gown,
Sewn with sequins and blue bows.
And on her feet glass slippers shone,
With heels both thin and high;
While round her neck hung diamonds
Only millionaires could buy.

"Oh wow! I look amazing,"
Cinderella cried in glee.
"But however shall I get there?
The buses stop at three."
"Go quickly find a pumpkin,"
Fairy Godmother replied.
"I'll conjure up a carriage
With red velvet seats inside."

"But must it be a carriage?"
Cinderella glumly said.
"I'd rather have a motor bike,
Or motor car instead.
A horse can't move as quickly
As a high-performance car.
If you could grant me one request:
An F-Type Jaguar?"

"Oh very well," the Fairy said;
Then after half a minute,
A smart red Jaguar appeared,
And Cinders stepped straight in it.
"Now one last thing," the Fairy warned,
"Be careful of the time,
For all of this will disappear
When midnight starts to chime."

Off to the palace Cinders roared,
Arriving there at eight,
And people stood and gasped and stared,
As she drove through the gate.
"Who is that girl?" Prince Charming cried,
"I must ask her for a dance,
For she is fair as fair can be –
The picture of romance."

And so just moments later,
They were waltzing round the floor,
But Cinders quickly realised
Prince Charming was a bore.
What's more he had no rhythm,
As a dancer he was grim.
"I'd have to be stark mad," she thought,
"To go and marry him."

But what was the alternative?
Go home and be a slave?
Then suddenly from out the blue –
A genius brainwave!
She said, "Oh Prince, I need a rest,
For dancing in glass shoes
Is actually quite painful
And has given me a bruise."

So kicking off the slippers,
She grabbed the Prince's hand,
And said, "Come see my sports car!
It's the fastest in the land."

Now when Prince Charming saw it,
He was really blown away.
He cried, "I'll buy it from you.
Name your price and I will pay!"
So Cinders said, "A million pounds,
Including VAT."
The Prince produced the cash and said,
"Sounds fair enough to me."
And straight away, without a pause,

He zoomed off out of sight.
Then crafty Cinderella smiled –
"Not long now till midnight.
My gorgeous clothes will disappear,
The Prince's car will too,
But as for happy endings – well –
This million quid will do!"

Welcome to our famous

Troll Bistro

Soup of the day:
Twelve Elephants

Join us right now!

Grandma's
Boxing Club

ROYAL PEAS
1568

HELPING TO CERTIFY
A PRINCESS
SINCE 1568

WE
RECOMMEND

ELF & ELF
FOOTWEAR

GENUINE LEATHER

Hair Extension
"RAPUNZEL'S JOKE"

**TRY IT NOW!
SURPRISE
A WITCH!**

CBB

TIP-TOP GEAR

Just three steps to owning your new F-Type Jaguar

Step 1. Find a pumpkin

Step 2. Call a fairy

Step 3. Ready!

Keep in mind that it will disappear when midnight